The Case Of The
Nutcracker Ballet

Look for more great books in

The New Adventures of

MARY-KATE & ASHLEY™

series:

The Case Of The Great Elephant Escape
The Case Of The Summer Camp Caper
The Case Of The Surfing Secret
The Case Of The Green Ghost
The Case Of The Big Scare Mountain Mystery
The Case Of The Slam Dunk Mystery
The Case Of The Rock Star's Secret
The Case Of The Cheerleading Camp Mystery
The Case Of The Flying Phantom
The Case Of The Creepy Castle
The Case Of The Golden Slipper
The Case Of The Flapper 'Napper
The Case Of The High Seas Secret
The Case Of The Logical I Ranch
The Case Of The Dog Camp Mystery
The Case Of The Screaming Scarecrow
The Case Of The Jingle Bell Jinx
The Case Of The Game Show Mystery
The Case Of The Mall Mystery
The Case Of The Weird Science Mystery
The Case Of Camp Crooked Lake
The Case Of The Giggling Ghost
The Case Of The Candy Cane Clue
The Case Of The Hollywood Who-Done-It
The Case Of The Sundae Surprise
The Case Of Clue's Circus Caper
The Case Of Camp Pom-Pom
The Case Of The Tattooed Cat

and coming soon

The Case Of The Clue At The Zoo

The Case Of The
Nutcracker Ballet

by Megan Stine

HarperEntertainment
An Imprint of HarperCollins*Publishers*

A PARACHUTE PRESS BOOK

PARACHUTE PRESS

Parachute Publishing, L.L.C.
156 Fifth Avenue
New York, NY 10010

DUALSTAR PUBLICATIONS

Dualstar Publications
c/o Thorne and Company
A Professional Law Corporation
1801 Century Park East
Los Angeles, CA 90067

HarperEntertainment

An Imprint of HarperCollins*Publishers*
10 East 53rd Street, New York, NY 10022

10 9 8 7 6 5 4 3 2 1

1

Rehearsal Time

"**A**shley, you're dancing in *The Nutcracker* ballet *tomorrow*!" I said to my twin sister. "You're practically famous!"

I was sitting with Ashley and our friend Sarah in a corner of Madame Pavlova's dance studio. Ashley's ballet class practiced there every week. Tomorrow they would perform in the Pavlova Theater right next door!

"Come on, Mary-Kate." Ashley blushed.

"I have a *small* part in the ballet. But I love being in the show."

"I wish I could be in the show too," Sarah said. She twirled a lock of her brown hair around her finger. "But I can't—all because of my dopey brother Noah!"

Sarah is nine, a year younger than Ashley and me. She's in the same dance class as Ashley. Today she carried crutches and had a cast on her right ankle.

"What happened?" I asked.

"Noah put a frog in my ballet bag. I jumped and tripped over our cat, Mr. Snuffles. I sprained my ankle, so I can't dance. And Mr. Snuffles is a nervous wreck!" Sarah sighed. "If I can't be in the ballet, I'm glad you are, Ashley. Are you nervous?"

"Well, maybe a little," Ashley admitted. She tightened the ribbons on her ballet slippers and stretched out her legs. "But I'll feel better once we get to practice onstage in our costumes."

"Dancers, take your places, please." Madame Pavlova clapped her hands.

Madame Pavlova has pale, smooth skin and big brown eyes. Her black hair was wrapped tightly in a bun. "I want to run through the Christmas-party dance before we go to the theater. And I want no mistakes this time!"

"Maybe I should be glad I'm not spending my Christmas vacation performing in the ballet," Sarah said. "Madame P. can be pretty tough!"

"Madame P.?" I giggled. "Why do you call her that?"

"That's what we call Madame Pavlova for short," Ashley explained. "She *is* strict, but she's a great teacher."

Madame Pavlova clapped her hands again.

"See you guys later!" Ashley said. She rushed to join the other dancers in the center of the room.

Ashley and I both have strawberry-blond hair and blue eyes. But Ashley is the graceful one in the family. *I* would much rather wear a baseball uniform than a tutu. But I love watching Ashley dance. I couldn't wait to see her in The *Nutcracker*!

At least I get to help out with the ballet. I'm going to be an usher at tomorrow night's performance. It will be fun to wear a red uniform and show people to their seats.

Sarah stood up and grabbed her crutches. "I'll see you later, Mary-Kate," she said. "My mom's taking me to the doctor. I'll be back to watch the dress rehearsal."

"See you!" I said. I took a seat against the wall. The dancers stood in place on the gleaming wood floor. They all wore black leotards and tights.

Madame Pavlova turned on the music. "Let's begin!" she said.

Ashley and the other girls and boys began to dance. They pretended to be at a Christmas party. A twelve-year-old girl danced through the center of the crowd. She wore her long red hair in a neat French braid. It was Miranda, the star of the ballet. She played the role of Clara.

Miranda twirled with her arms above her head. She lifted her leg high and—

"Ow!" Miranda cried. She fell to the floor.

Madame Pavlova stopped the music. "Are you all right, Miranda?" she asked.

A girl with curly blond hair giggled. "I *told* you she dances like an elephant," Becky said. "Maybe I should play Clara, and Miranda can be *my* understudy."

Becky was furious when Madame Pavlova gave the part of Clara to Miranda and made her Miranda's understudy. That meant that if Miranda couldn't dance in the ballet tomorrow night, Becky would take her place as Clara.

Miranda got up. "You pushed me!" she yelled at Becky.

"Did not!" Becky said.

"Did too!" Miranda replied angrily.

"Quiet!" Madame Pavlova shouted. She looked at Becky. "Excuse me, Becky, but what is that shiny blue stuff all over your arms?"

"It's body glitter," Becky said.

Madame P. pointed at the door. "Go wash it off! No makeup of any kind is allowed in class."

Becky frowned and stomped out of the room.

Madame Pavlova put a hand to her forehead. "There will be no more fighting in my ballet or *nobody* will dance tomorrow! Now let's begin again," she said.

The dancers took their places. The music started up again. Just then I heard a shout from the hall.

"Gotcha!" a boy yelled.

"You missed!" another boy yelled back.

I looked out the doorway and saw two boys playing with wooden swords. They were already wearing their costumes. I recognized the boy with wavy brown hair. It was Sarah's brother, Noah.

"Ha! Gotcha again!" Noah said. He was dressed in the costume of the Nutcracker Prince. He wore a white jacket with gold buttons and black pants. His white shirt hung out of his jacket.

"No way!" the other boy said. His name was Peter. He was dressed as a toy soldier. He wore a red jacket and white pants.

Peter stabbed at Noah's jacket. "Gotcha last! Gotcha last!" he cried.

I shook my head. Noah and Peter are both

eleven. But sometimes they act like babies!

Peter rushed past me into the studio. He ran so fast he tripped right over my chair!

"Oof!" Peter's wooden sword slid out of his hand and across the floor. It landed at Madame Pavlova's feet.

"Stop!" Madame Pavlova cried. "Stop! Stop! Stop!"

The dancers froze.

Madame Pavlova turned to Peter and Noah. "Noah! Peter! Look what you have done to your costumes. They are a mess!"

Peter's face turned red. "Sorry," he mumbled.

"Come on, Madame P." Noah grinned at her. "We were just having fun!"

"Now is not the time for fun! We have a show to put on," Madame Pavlova scolded. "I want the two of you cleaned up and ready for dress rehearsal. It begins in fifteen minutes. Do you understand?"

"Yes," the boys said. As they walked out of the room, Noah made a face behind Madame Pavlova's back.

Madame Pavlova looked at the rest of the dancers. "I want all of you to go to the dressing rooms and change into your costumes. Then we'll go to the theater for dress rehearsal," she told them.

I caught up to Ashley at the door. She was talking to Miranda.

"Becky did push me," Miranda was saying, "but I don't care. Madame Pavlova knows I'm a good dancer. And I'm going to do great tomorrow."

"You're always so sure of yourself," Ashley said. "What's your secret?"

Miranda smiled. "I'm going to wear my lucky ballet slippers."

Everyone knows about Miranda's ballet slippers. She wears them for every performance. She says they help her dance her best.

"Do you guys need help with your costumes?" I asked. I knew Ashley's dress had a tricky zipper.

Ashley nodded. We walked down the hall to the girls' dressing room. Everyone was buzzing with excitement.

"I'll see you guys in a few minutes." Miranda squeezed her way to the back of the dressing room.

Ashley took her costume off the rack and put it on. I helped her zip it up. "Thanks, Mary-Ka—" Ashley started to say.

That's when we heard a terrible scream.

"Oh, no!" Miranda cried. "My lucky ballet slippers are gone!"

2

THE STOLEN SLIPPERS

Ashley and I ran to the back of the dressing room. All the other girls crowded around Miranda. Everyone except Becky.

"What happened?" Ashley asked Miranda.

"Someone stole my lucky ballet slippers!" Miranda cried.

"Oh, no!" A girl named Ariel gasped. "Not your lucky lavender slippers!"

Ariel is one of the younger dancers in the class. She is always hanging around with Miranda. She really looks up to her.

"Yes!" Miranda wailed. "The ones I had dyed to match Danielle Dabro's."

I had heard that name before. Danielle Dabro is a famous ballerina. She was once a student at Madame Pavlova's school. She danced the part of Clara years ago.

I turned to Ashley. "I thought ballet shoes had to be pink."

"Danielle Dabro always wore lavender shoes when she danced at the school," Ashley said. "A pair of her slippers are for sale in the gift shop. And they're signed by Danielle too."

Becky walked over. "What's all the racket, Miranda?" she asked. "Did you trip over your own feet again?"

"Her lucky ballet slippers are missing," Ariel told her.

"You probably just left them at home," Becky said.

"No, I brought them with me," Miranda insisted. "I wanted to wear them for the dress rehearsal." She looked at Ashley and me. "You two are detectives. Can you help me find them?"

Ashley and I run the Olsen and Olsen Detective Agency out of the attic of our house. We have a silent partner—a basset hound named Clue. If she were here, she could help us sniff out the slippers fast.

I looked at Ashley. She gave me the thumbs-up. "We'll take the case," I told Miranda.

Miranda smiled. "That would be great!"

Madame Pavlova poked her head into the room. "What's going on?" she asked. "Why isn't anyone getting dressed! Rehearsal starts in ten minutes!"

Everyone hurried to finish getting into their costumes. One by one, the girls got dressed and left.

"No time to look for clues," Ashley said.

"Do you want me to check the dressing room while you're onstage?" I asked.

Ashley thought about it. "Maybe you should keep an eye on the rehearsal instead. Make sure nothing else funny happens. We can check the dressing room later."

I nodded. Ashley has a very logical mind. She's good at thinking up a plan.

Ashley and I walked down the hallway that connects the theater to the dance school. The dancers hurried onto the stage. I sat down in one of the red velvet seats in the audience. I had a great view of the action.

I was excited for the rehearsal to start—and not just because we had a mystery to solve. I love *The Nutcracker* ballet. The story takes place on Christmas Eve. A girl named Clara falls asleep, and amazing things happen. Her nutcracker doll comes to life and fights an army of mice. She meets the Sugar Plum Fairy and a handsome prince. It's very magical.

A huge Christmas tree stood in the center of the stage. Lots of presents were piled underneath it. The dancers came onstage. At Madame P.'s signal, they began to dance.

The dancers seemed to be doing great—until Madame Pavlova clapped her hands and yelled, "No, no!" The music stopped.

"Noah, come here." Madame P. strode onto the stage. She bent her head and stared at Noah's white jacket. "What happened to your costume? You've lost a button!"

"Huh?" Noah glanced down. One of the gold buttons was missing from the front of his jacket.

"How did you lose it?" Madame P. asked.

"Maybe the Sugar Plum Fairy took it," Noah said with a grin.

"Oh, Noah, that's the third button you've lost. What am I going to do with you?" Madame P. sounded tired. "Go ask Nadia to sew on another button."

"Excuse me, Madame P." A short woman walked onto the stage. She wore a blue smock with ribbons and pins stuck all over it. "We don't have any more buttons for that costume."

It was Nadia, the costume designer for the show.

"Then we must find the one Noah lost," Madame Pavlova said. "Those are specially made buttons. They have the Nutcracker Prince's crown stamped on them. No other button will match!"

"Do you want me to look for it?" Nadia offered.

"Yes, please. And hurry!" Madame P. replied. Then she turned to the dancers. "All right. Let's begin again."

The music started up, and all the party guests ran to look at the Christmas tree. Miranda bumped into Ashley and almost knocked her over.

Uh-oh, I thought. That wasn't supposed to happen.

In the next scene, Peter started to chase Miranda. But she forgot to run. She just stood there—and Peter smacked right into her!

"Stop! Stop!" Madame P. said. "Miranda! Are you all right?"

Miranda didn't say anything. She stood still for a minute, her face turning red. Her eyes filled with tears. Then she ran off the stage!

"Oh, dear," Madame P. said. She sighed. "All right, everyone. Let's take a break."

"Come on, Ashley!" I called. "Let's see if we can help."

We rushed after Madame P. to the dress-

ing room. Miranda was sitting in a heap on the floor. Her face was red from crying.

"What's wrong, Miranda?" Madame P. asked in a soft voice.

"It's my shoes," Miranda explained. "My lucky ballet slippers are gone. And now I can't concentrate on my dancing!"

Madame P. patted Miranda's shoulder. "I know how that is. I had a pair of lucky shoes myself when I was a young dancer."

"You did?" Miranda's eyes opened wide.

"Yes," Madame P. said. "But luck isn't why you have the part of Clara. You are a wonderful dancer—with or without your lucky slippers."

Miranda gulped. "But I *need* my slippers," she said. "Mary-Kate and Ashley are going to help me find them. They are detectives."

"Good," Madame P. said. "But you must still be able to rehearse today. The show goes on tomorrow, and I am depending on you. Now, dry your eyes and come back to rehearsal."

Madame P. hurried back to the stage. We sat down next to Miranda.

"Tell us, Miranda," Ashley said. "Exactly where were your ballet slippers when they were stolen?"

"They were in my ballet bag," Miranda said, wiping her eyes. "I was late to class this morning. I didn't have time to put the bag in my locker. I left it out on the bench."

I looked around the room. The room was divided into rows by metal lockers. In the middle of each row was a wooden bench. Miranda's black ballet bag sat on the bench in front of her locker.

"Are you *sure* you brought the slippers with you to class?" I asked.

"I always keep them in my bag, even if I'm not going to wear them," Miranda said.

Ashley bent down beside Miranda's bag.

I knelt beside her. The zipper was unzipped, and the bag gaped open.

Everything looked normal. There was a pair of rolled-up socks. A hairbrush. A small mirror.

Then I saw something—something that didn't belong.

"Do you see what I see?" Ashley asked.

I jumped up and down. "It's a clue!"

3

A SHINY CLUE

"**I**t looks like glitter," I said. "Blue glitter!"

I pulled a small plastic bag and a paint-brush out of our detective backpack. Ashley and I always carry it with us. Our great-grandma Olive is a world-famous detective. She taught us to always be prepared.

Ashley took the paintbrush and carefully brushed the glitter into the bag.

"Whoever took the shoes must have been wearing glitter," I said.

Ashley scrunched up her eyebrows. She always does that when she's thinking hard.

"Miranda, you said your shoes were in your bag this morning," she said. "We had rehearsal. Then you checked your bag and the shoes were gone. So the shoes must have been stolen during rehearsal."

"Right." I nodded. "By someone wearing blue glitter—"

We all had the same thought. "Becky!" we cried out.

"She was wearing blue body glitter at rehearsal," I said. "And she left rehearsal early to take it off."

"And Becky has a reason to steal the slippers," Ashley pointed out. "She knows Miranda can't dance without her lucky slippers. If Miranda messes up—"

"—then Becky gets the part of Clara!" I finished. "She must have done it!"

I jumped up. Case closed!

"Hang on," Ashley said. "Becky is a suspect. But we have no proof. We need to find some." She wrote Becky's name in her detective notebook.

Miranda was frowning. "I bet it *was* Becky!" she said. "This is so not fair!"

Nadia rushed into the room. "Miranda, you're supposed to be onstage," she said. "Go!"

Miranda sighed and went back to rehearsal.

"Have you girls seen the Mouse King's sword?" Nadia asked us. "I can't find it anywhere!"

"No," Ashley said, "but may I ask you a question?"

"What is it?" Nadia asked. She searched under a pile of clothes. Dancers' costumes were in piles all over the room.

"Did you see Becky in here this morning?" Ashley asked.

Nadia shook her head. "No. I spent all morning trying to find the Mouse King's sword!"

"Could you please look at this glitter?" Ashley asked Nadia. She showed her the plastic bag.

Nadia looked up. She brushed a strand of blond hair from her face. "What about it?" she asked.

"We think it's body glitter. Do you know any other dancers besides Becky who wear it?" Ashley asked.

"I don't think so," Nadia said. "But maybe it's not body glitter. Maybe it fell off one of the costumes."

Fell off a costume? I hadn't thought of that. "Whose costume?" I asked.

"Who knows," Nadia said. "All the girls who dance with the Sugar Plum Fairy have blue glitter on their costumes."

Nadia turned over one last pile of

clothes. Then she left the dressing room, shaking her head.

"Hmm," I said, thinking hard. "I guess the case isn't closed. Let's think . . . who dances with the Sugar Plum Fairy?"

Ashley thought for a moment. "Ariel!" she announced. "She wants to be just like Miranda."

"Yes," I agreed. "She wears her hair like Miranda. Maybe she wants shoes like Miranda's too."

She shook her head. "Ariel and Miranda are friends. I don't think Ariel would do anything to hurt Miranda."

She had a point. "I still think Becky is our number one suspect," I said. "But let's put Ariel on the list, just in case."

Ashley nodded. She wrote Ariel's name on the suspect list. Then we hurried back to the stage.

Ashley was just in time. The dancers

playing party guests were lining up again. The dance began.

The dancers twirled. Noah leaped around on a wooden horse. Peter chased him as the music played.

Everyone danced well. Everyone but Miranda, that is. She was out of step with the other dancers. The more she messed up, the more upset she looked. Then she bumped into Noah and Peter by mistake.

Madame Pavlova stopped the music. She walked up to Miranda and led her to one side of the stage. She and Miranda talked. Miranda looked like she was going to cry again.

Madame Pavlova turned back to the dancers. "We will take a short break," she said.

The dancers left the stage. I walked up to Ashley.

"Let's talk to Becky now," I said.

Ashley nodded. We found Becky sitting on the edge of the stage.

"Becky," I said, "can we show you something?"

Becky was breathing hard from dancing. "What?"

"This," Ashley said. She held up the bag with the tiny bit of blue glitter in it. "We found this on Miranda's dance bag."

Becky squinted. "What is it?" she asked.

"It's blue glitter," Ashley said. "We think the person who stole Miranda's ballet shoes got blue glitter on her dance bag."

"Well, don't look at me!" Becky said with a huff. "I didn't touch her stupid bag. *Or* her lucky shoes!"

She tossed her hair over her shoulders and pranced off.

"I don't believe her," I told Ashley. "She tripped Miranda before. She *really* wants the part of Clara."

"That's true," Ashley said. "But we still don't have solid proof. Maybe we should talk to our other suspect."

Ariel wasn't hard to find. She was backstage watching Miranda, who was practicing onstage with Madame Pavlova.

Ariel leaned against a giant lollipop made out of wood. The backstage area was crowded with large wood pieces painted to look like candy. They would be used later in the ballet to decorate the stage for the Sugar Plum Fairy's dance.

"We need to talk to you," I said. "Did you leave the rehearsal studio at all this morning?"

Ariel shrugged. "Sure. I left my costume at home. My mom dropped it off, and I brought it to the dressing room. Why?"

I looked at Ashley. If Ariel had been in the dressing room alone, then she had had the chance to steal Miranda's shoes.

"Was anyone else in the dressing room with you?" I asked.

Ariel shook her head. "Nope—only me."

I took a deep breath. "Just one more question," I said. "Ariel, did you take anything from Miranda's ballet bag this morning?"

Ariel looked away. She stared at her feet for a minute, then looked up at us.

I held my breath. Was Ariel about to confess?

"Yes," Ariel said. "I did take something from Miranda's bag. How did you know?"

4

MIRANDA'S BAD LUCK

I couldn't believe it. Had we solved the mystery already?

"I'm sorry," Ariel said quickly. "I thought it would be okay. Miranda said I could borrow them some time."

"Miranda said you could borrow her lucky ballet slippers?" I gasped.

"No!" Ariel cried. "Her hair clips! I would never take her lucky slippers."

"Hair clips?" I asked. "What hair clips?"

"Miranda has these really pretty hair clips. They're shaped like hearts," Ariel explained. "She said I could borrow them. When I brought my costume from the car, I saw them in her bag. So I thought, why not borrow them now?"

Nadia stuck her head backstage.

"Ariel, Madame P. is looking for you!" she said.

Ariel ran off, and Ashley and I looked at each other.

"Do you believe her?" Ashley asked.

I shrugged. "I'm not sure. She *sounds* like she's telling the truth."

"But she might be lying," Ashley pointed out. "And her costume does have blue glitter on it."

"I know," I said. "Look, there's glitter on the floor!"

I bent down to look at the glitter from Ariel's costume. I took another plastic evi-

dence bag out of my backpack and brushed the glitter into it.

Ashley pulled out the bag with the blue glitter from Miranda's ballet bag.

We peered at the two plastic bags. The glitter from Ariel's costume was in big chunks. The glitter from Miranda's bag was tiny little sparkles.

"Ariel's glitter is not like the glitter we found on Miranda's bag," I announced.

"That means we can cross Ariel off our suspect list," Ashley said.

"What now?" I asked.

Ashley thought. "We need to do some more work on this case. We need to think about who else had a chance to steal the shoes."

I understood. "Right. We know Miranda's shoes were stolen during rehearsal this morning."

"Exactly," Ashley said. "We need to ask

around and find out if anyone else left rehearsal."

I thought back to that morning. "Sarah left early," I said. "Her mom came to get her for a doctor's appointment."

"That's true, but I don't think she would take Miranda's slippers," Ashley said.

I remembered something else. "Noah and Peter! They were fooling around in the hallway, remember? They could have gone into the dressing room."

As soon as I said it, I felt silly. What would a boy want with Miranda's ballet shoes?

"We'll put them on the suspect list," Ashley said, writing down their names. "But I don't think either of them had a reason to do it."

I leaned against a giant candy cane and sighed. This case was going nowhere. We had no proof against Becky, our main sus-

pect. And our other suspects weren't very good.

Madame Pavlova's voice rang through the theater. "Everyone back to the stage!" she called.

"How can we get any work done when you're always dancing?" I said.

"Don't worry," Ashley said. "We have a lunch break soon. We'll do some detecting then."

I nodded. Ashley rushed back to the stage. I headed back to my seat in the audience. I planned on keeping my eyes and ears open for any more clues.

On the stage, Madame Pavlova was yelling at Noah. "Noah! Your button is still missing! Didn't you find it yet?"

Noah shook his head. "Come on, Madame P. Being a prince takes a lot of work!"

Madame Pavlova took a deep breath.

"All right," she said. "Let's start with Clara's entrance."

The music began to play, and Miranda danced gracefully onto the stage. But as she whirled past Becky, she stumbled.

"Miranda, keep your head up, please," Madame Pavlova called over the music.

Miranda cringed. On her next step, she tripped and fell.

Madame Pavlova shook her head. "We'd better stop for lunch now," she said. "Miranda, Becky, may I speak to you for a minute?"

The dancers hurried offstage and headed for the lunchroom in the rehearsal studio.

Ashley and I waited by the door for Miranda. After a few minutes, she came rushing toward us. Tears streamed down her face.

"Miranda, what's wrong?" Ashley asked.

"Madame P. says I'm too nervous. She

told me to take a break," she said. "She wants Becky to dance the part of Clara at the rehearsal after lunch."

"Oh, no!" I cried.

"Don't worry," Ashley said. "It's just a break. You'll get over your nerves before tomorrow night."

Miranda shook her head. "It's impossible. I can't dance without my lucky slippers!" Then she ran down the hallway.

Becky danced up to us. She had a huge smile on her face.

"Too bad about Miranda," she said. "Once Madame P. sees me dance at rehearsal, she'll let me dance the part of Clara tomorrow!"

I turned to Ashley.

"That settles it," I said. "We've got to solve this mystery—fast!"

5

A CLUE IN THE TRASH

Ashley and I stared at Becky as she walked away.

"She's guilty. I just *know* it," I said to Ashley.

"I think so too," Ashley agreed. She looked at her watch. "It's lunchtime. Let's watch Becky and see if we can get some proof."

Ashley and I followed Becky and the other dancers to the lunchroom. It is a

large room behind the rehearsal studio. Posters of dancers hang on the white walls. Long tables fill the room.

We watched Becky as she sat down with some friends at a table next to the door. Ashley and I sat down at the table next to Becky's. We wanted to keep her in sight.

I pulled a peanut-butter-and-jelly sandwich out of my backpack and took a bite. Miranda and Ariel came and sat at our table.

Miranda took a tuna-fish sandwich from her bag and stared at it. "I can't eat," she said. She glanced at the table where Becky was eating lunch.

"I *know* Becky took my shoes," Miranda said. "She's probably *trying* to make me have bad luck and mess up so she can play Clara!"

"Can I have your sandwich if you don't want it?" Peter asked. He and Noah stood behind Miranda. He grabbed for her sandwich.

"Sure." Miranda nodded glumly. Her shoulders slumped.

"Who wants my yogurt?" Ariel asked.

"I'll take it!" Noah yelled, lunging for the cup. Both boys sat down at our table and began to eat.

I took a bite of my sandwich and continued to watch Becky. She was making a list of her friends who were coming to opening night. "They'll all see me dance!" she announced loudly.

I turned to Ashley and whispered, "Not if we catch her with the stolen shoes!"

"If Becky does have the shoes, where are they?" Ashley asked.

"We need to search her locker," I whispered back. "We'll have to go back to the dressing room."

"Don't forget, we wanted to talk to Peter

and Noah too," Ashley reminded me. "And here they are!"

Before we had a chance to say anything to Peter and Noah, Nadia rushed in. She was carrying the Mouse King's sword. "I finally found it!"

"Where was it?" Ashley said.

"It was stuck between some wooden boxes backstage," Nadia answered. "I don't know how it got there." She looked at Noah and Peter.

"Maybe one of the mice used it to cut a slice of cheese," Noah said.

Peter laughed so hard, milk spurted out of his nose.

Nadia shook her finger at Noah. "Noah, stop joking around! It's bad enough you lost your button. I need you to help me look for it."

"I haven't finished eating yet, Nadia," Noah said. "I need to keep up my strength."

Nadia frowned. Then she glanced at Ashley and me. "Maybe I should hire you two to solve the case of the missing button!"

"Sorry, Nadia, but we're already on the case of the missing slippers!" I told her.

"Too bad," Nadia said. She hurried out of the room.

Ashley turned to me. "Maybe now would be a good time to talk to Noah and Peter."

I nodded. But before I could say a word, Peter wadded up his napkin and threw it at Noah. "Come on!" he said. "Let's go outside!"

Noah tossed the napkin back. "I'm still eating."

Peter grabbed two more napkins and balled them up. "He shoots! He scores!" he shouted as the wads hit Noah on the head.

"I'll get you for that!" Noah cried. He balled up three napkins and two pieces of paper and hurled them at Peter.

"Hey!" I cried. I ducked too late. A nap-

kin hit me on the head. A glob of jelly fell on my hair.

"Watch it, Noah!" I yelled. I threw the napkin back at Noah—but he ducked. It hit Becky instead!

Becky gasped. The napkin still had some jelly in it. The jelly oozed out of the napkin and onto one of Becky's perfect blond curls.

"You are in big trouble now, Mary-Kate!" Becky said. She lobbed her brown paper lunch bag at me.

Pretty soon, half the kids in the lunchroom were throwing wadded-up napkins. Even Ashley!

Ariel picked up a napkin and pretended to throw it at Peter—but she was really aiming it at Becky. The napkin hit Becky right in the face.

"Oops, sorry." Ariel smiled sweetly at her. Becky glared at Ariel.

"What is going on in here!" a loud voice yelled. It was Madame P. She walked into the middle of the lunchroom. A napkin hit her right on the forehead.

"Girls! Boys!" she shouted, clapping her hands. "Stop this right now!"

Everyone froze. The room grew quiet.

"This is not how young dancers behave!" Madame P. said. "I want you all to clean this up—fast! Then return to the stage immediately. Rehearsal begins again in ten minutes!"

Peter and Noah each picked up just one piece of paper and tossed it into the garbage can. Then they ran out.

"Oh, great," I said. "They left all the work for us!"

Becky glared at me. "I can't clean up. I need to get this jelly out of my hair before rehearsal." She stormed out of the lunch-room.

"Do you believe her?" I asked. "I got jelly in my hair too." I went to the water fountain and washed out the jelly.

All of the kids began cleaning up. But soon Ashley and I were the only ones left. I picked up the last piece of paper. I was about to throw it out when something caught my eye.

"Hey," I said. "What's this?"

The paper had writing all over it—in blue glitter ink! Was it a clue?

I opened the balled-up piece of paper and gasped. Someone had written the name 'Danielle Dabro' over and over again!

"Ashley, look!" I said. "Do you think this has something to do with Miranda's missing ballet slippers?"

6

THE MYSTERY BOY

Ashley and I stared at the piece of note-book paper. The name 'Danielle Dabro' was written six or seven times on the page.

"How weird!" Ashley said. "Miranda's lucky shoes were just like Danielle Dabro's. And now we find a piece of paper with Danielle Dabro's name all over it!"

"This *has* to be a clue!" I said. "But why would someone write Danielle Dabro's name over and over?"

"I don't know," Ashley said. "I think we need to go to the gift shop to find out."

I snapped my fingers. "You're right! Danielle Dabro's autographed ballet slippers are on sale at the gift shop! Great idea, Ashley! But don't you need to be at rehearsal?"

"I'm not in this scene," Ashley said, "so I have time for some detecting. But let's not rush into things, Mary-Kate. We still need to search Becky's locker for the missing slippers."

I grinned at Ashley. "I got so excited when I found this new clue, I almost forgot!"

We left the lunchroom and walked to the girls' dressing room. Most of the lockers were open. Dance bags sat on the benches. Each locker had a name on it. We looked around until we found Becky's.

"It's locked!" I said. "I wonder if it's because Miranda's lucky slippers are in there."

"Well, there isn't anything else we can do here," Ashley said. "Let's go to the gift shop!"

We left the dressing room and went over to the theater. Most of the other dancers were onstage. Ashley and I hurried through the theater lobby. We opened the glass door to the gift shop.

Music from *The Nutcracker* ballet played through speakers on the wall. Racks of sheet music and CDs were lined up next to the counter. T-shirts, hats, and leotards hung from hooks and hangers. A glass cabinet held the more valuable items.

"Hello, girls," a woman with gray hair said. "May I help you?"

"Hi," I said. "We came to see Danielle Dabro's autographed ballet slippers."

"Oh." The woman frowned. "I'm sorry, but those slippers were sold this morning. They're gone."

"Gone?" Ashley and I stared at each other.

"Who bought them?" I asked. Maybe this would help us with our case.

"Oh, um . . . hmm. I can't remember," the woman said. She fiddled with a pencil. "Would you like to see something else?"

"You can't remember?" I repeated. That sounded pretty fishy to me. It was only this morning, after all!

"No, I can't," she said. "But they *were* lovely shoes. And expensive! They sold for two-hundred nineteen dollars because February 19 is Danielle Dabro's birthday. That was her lucky number."

"Wow." Ashley whistled. "That's a lot of money."

"Yes, it is," the woman said. "And you're the second person to come in asking about them today."

I clutched Ashley's arm. That sounded like a clue! "Who else came in?" I asked.

"A young boy," the woman said. "He seemed really upset that they were gone. He said he had ruined everything—again! I can't imagine what he was talking about."

"A boy? That's weird. Why would a *boy* want girl's ballet slippers?" I asked. "Do you know who the boy was?"

The woman shrugged. "I don't know his name," she said, "but he had brown hair."

My eyes lit up. "Noah and Peter *both* have brown hair!"

"I know," Ashley agreed. "But you're right—why would a boy want a pair of girl's ballet slippers? And what does it have to do with Miranda's shoes, anyway?"

I couldn't think of an answer for that.

Ashley gasped. "I've got to get back!"

We ran back to the theater. Ashley joined the other dancers on the stage.

I sat in a chair in the first row of the theater and watched. Half an hour later,

Madame Pavlova clapped her hands.

"Rehearsal is over for now," she told the dancers. "I need to consult with some of the dancers. After that, I would like to have a meeting to discuss the show. I want everyone to meet in the rehearsal room in half an hour."

Madame P. took Becky and Miranda to the dance studio's rehearsal room. The other dancers left the theater. We searched the crowd for Noah and Peter, but we couldn't see either of them. Then the stage lights went off. The only light in the theater came from old-fashioned lamps on the walls.

"Noah and Peter must be around somewhere," Ashley said. "We never did get to talk to them. And now it's really important. One of them could be the boy from the gift shop."

We headed down the aisle toward the

stage. A large cloth curtain hung in front of the scenery. A snow scene was painted on it. Happy children played under a sky of twirling snowflakes.

The theater was quiet except for the sound of our footsteps. Then Ashley and I heard a strange noise—a loud rustling. It came from behind the cloth. We stopped and looked around.

We heard a click—and suddenly all the stage lights came on.

"Mary-Kate, look!" Ashley gasped.

My mouth dropped open. Behind the cloth, we could see the shadow of a boy crossing the stage—and I was sure he was carrying a pair of girl's ballet slippers!

7

A Chase in the Dark

"**H**ey! Stop!" Ashley cried.

We ran toward the stage. The boy behind the cloth ran too. He was definitely carrying ballet slippers. We could see the long ribbons. But we couldn't tell who he was.

Ashley and I rushed up the steps to the stage. The boy darted behind a pile of Christmas presents.

"We've got him," I said.

But suddenly there was another loud

click, and the lights onstage went out again!

"Oh, no!" Ashley cried. I stopped short and bumped into her.

The boy ran out from behind the presents, knocking them down. Then he dashed behind the giant Christmas tree.

Who is it? I wondered. In the dark, I still couldn't tell. *Peter? Noah? Or another boy?*

"Shhh . . ." Ashley grabbed my hand. "Maybe we can sneak up on him," she whispered.

Step by step, Ashley and I tiptoed toward the tree. We were inches away from it when—

"There he goes!" Ashley cried.

The boy must have heard us coming. He ran across the stage. This time, he dashed into a huge wooden box. It was painted to look like a Christmas present.

"Get him!" I called, running into the box.

The box was hinged on all sides. I saw the dark figure push open the back panel. Then he darted away.

"Where did he go?" Ashley called.

I whirled around and came out of the box. "He went backstage!"

Ashley and I ran behind the big wall of the scenery. The only light in the backstage area came from a bare bulb over the emergency exit.

The giant pieces of candy looked like a strange forest in the darkness. I knew the boy had to be hiding behind one of them. But which one?

I held my breath and crept toward a giant lollipop.

"Ashley," I whispered. "Maybe he's here."

There was no answer.

I turned around. I couldn't see Ashley anywhere! I turned back to the lollipop. Then I quickly ran behind it.

There was no one there. I let out a breath. The boy must be hiding somewhere else.

I heard something behind me. Someone moving. Breathing. "Who's there?" I whispered, my voice shaking.

No one answered. Then I felt something brush past my face!

"Ahh!" I screamed, and jumped.

"Ahh!" Ashley screamed beside me.

I could just make out Ashley's shadowy figure in the dark. I held out my hand, and she grabbed it.

"I got lost," she explained.

"It's pretty creepy back here," I said. "Do you think the boy's still here?"

"I haven't heard any more footsteps," Ashley said. "Let's keep looking."

A row of candy canes towered overhead. Ashley and I weaved through the them. We didn't see anyone.

A crack of light appeared in the back wall.

"The back door!" I cried. "He's getting away!"

Ashley and I ran toward the back door. We jumped over piles of wooden swords and ran around boxes of props.

A boy leaped out from behind a giant gumdrop, swinging a long wooden sword!

"Ashley, look out!" I screamed.

8

MIRANDA'S DECISION

Ashley screamed and ducked.

"Gotcha!" yelled the boy.

It was still dark, but I recognized him. It was Peter!

"Oops! Sorry!" he said. He lowered the sword.

I gave Ashley a look. Was Peter the boy we were chasing?

"What are you doing back here?" Ashley asked him.

"I was just pretending to be the Mouse King," he said. "It's a lot more fun than being a boring soldier."

Ashley eyed him closely. "So what did you do with the slippers?" she asked.

"What slippers?" Peter asked.

"The ballet slippers you were carrying a minute ago," Ashley said.

"The *girl's* ballet slippers," I added.

Peter made a face. "Huh? Are you two nuts? What would I want with some girl's ballet slippers?" He marched off swinging his sword.

Ashley looked at me. "Do you believe him?"

"He could be lying," I said.

"He's the same size as the boy we were chasing," Ashley said. "But I can't tell if it was him."

My shoulders slumped. "We don't have any proof," I said. "And time is running out."

"If Miranda doesn't get her slippers back, she'll be too nervous to dance," Ashley said. "Madame P. will let Becky dance the part for sure."

"That would be terrible!" I said. "Becky is our main suspect. If she stole Miranda's shoes, she shouldn't get to dance Miranda's part."

Ashley checked her watch. "It's almost time for Madame P.'s meeting. We'd better get back to the rehearsal room."

As we walked, we talked about the case.

"Let's take a look at our suspect list," Ashley said. She took out her detective notebook. "Becky has the best motive. And she had a chance to steal the shoes when she left class this morning."

"Plus we found blue body glitter like hers on Miranda's dance bag," I said.

"Right," Ashley said. "But we also have Noah and Peter on the list. And some

boy—we don't know who—was asking for Danielle Dabro's slippers in the gift shop."

"And Danielle Dabro's shoes look just like Miranda's!" I added.

We reached the rehearsal room. The dancers were sitting on the floor in front of Madame P. Ashley joined them. I was about to follow her, when I saw Sarah come in on her crutches.

"How's your ankle?" I asked.

"I've got to be on crutches for two more weeks!" Sarah moaned. "How's rehearsal going?"

"Not great," I said. "Miranda's been messing up." I told Sarah all about her missing slippers.

"That's awful!" Sarah cried. "Miranda's slippers were so pretty. Just like Danielle Dabro's."

She got a dreamy look on her face. "Did you see Danielle's slippers in the gift shop?

~The New Adventures of~ MARY-KATE & ASHLEY ™

DETECTIVE TRICK

BALLET ARM LANGUAGE

Detectives often use secret signals to send messages to each other from across the room. Here's a way to do it using the five basic arm positions in ballet. Each position stands for a different message:

First position means everything is OK.
Second position means something is wrong.
Third position means look over there.
Fourth position means follow that person.
Fifth position means come over here, quick!

First   Second   Third   Fourth   Fifth

mary-kateandashley.com
America Online keyword: mary-kateandashley

From
The Case Of The **Nutcracker Ballet**

~The New Adventures of~ MARY-KATE & ASHLEY ™

DETECTIVE TRICK

TELEPHONE CODE

Here is a fun code using the numbers on a telephone. Each number stands for one of the three letters on the key pad. Use the * key for the letter Q and the # for Z, since those letters don't appear on the telephone.

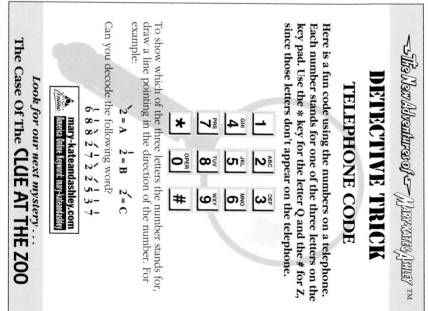

To show which of the three letters the number stands for, draw a line pointing in the direction of the number. For example:

2 = A   2 = B   2 = C

Can you decode the following word?

6 8 8 2 7 2 2 5 3 7

mary-kateandashley.com
America Online keyword: mary-kateandashley

Look for our next mystery...
The Case Of The **CLUE AT THE ZOO**

They're autographed and everything!"

Hmmm . . . so Sarah was a fan of Danielle Dabro's. . . . An idea started to form in my mind. If only I could talk to Ashley about it!

Sarah tugged on my arm. "Come on. I want to see what Madame P. has to say."

I followed Sarah into the rehearsal studio. We took seats against the wall.

"I have an announcement to make," Madame P. said. "Miranda has decided not to dance the role of Clara tomorrow. I am very sorry to hear this. I hope Miranda will change her mind."

Everyone was quiet. We all stared at Becky. She had a big smile on her face. Miranda was nowhere to be seen.

"So," Madame P. continued, "as of now, Becky will be dancing the role of Clara."

A few of the dancers clapped. Most of them looked upset.

"I will see you all tomorrow afternoon,"

Madame Pavlova finished. "Please get a good night's sleep. And remember to hang up your costumes!"

The dancers stood up. They started to whisper about Miranda. Ashley ran up to me.

"This is terrible!" she said. "We have to find Miranda."

We rushed to the girls' dressing room. Miranda was sitting on the bench.

"Miranda, what happened?" Ashley asked, sitting down beside her.

"It's no use," Miranda said. "I can't dance without my lucky slippers. I just can't!"

"Of course you can," Ashley said. "You're the best dancer in the class. You don't need your slippers to be good."

But Miranda just shook her head. "I know Becky took my slippers, and now she took my part!"

"This isn't over yet, Miranda," I said. "Come on, Ashley! Let's go find those slippers!"

Ashley nodded. We left Miranda and went to the boys' dressing room.

I peeked my head inside. It was empty.

"Perfect," Ashley said. "We can look for clues. Maybe the boy we saw with the slippers stashed them in here."

The boys' locker room was a mess! Towels and smelly socks were lying all over the place. We found Peter's locker first. It wasn't locked.

Inside were Peter's jacket and his dance bag. Inside his bag were shoes and a change of clothes, but nothing else.

Then we found Noah's locker. The door hung open and dirty clothes spilled out onto the floor.

I wrinkled my nose. "Detecting can be dirty work!" I said.

We peered inside. Ashley lifted up a sweatshirt. Underneath it we saw Noah's backpack.

"That would be a good place to hide ballet slippers," I said.

Ashley unzipped the backpack. We didn't see any slippers. But right on top was an envelope with Noah's name on it.

"What's that?" I asked.

"I don't know," Ashley said. She hesitated. "We shouldn't be snooping, but we have to solve this case."

She picked up the envelope and opened it. It was filled with money! Lots of money!

Ashley counted it quickly. "Wow!" she said. "Guess how much is here? Exactly two-hundred nineteen dollars!"

I gasped. "That's the same price as Danielle Dabro's shoes!"

THE MISSING BUTTON

"This is our biggest clue yet!" I said.

"What do you mean?" Ashley asked.

"Noah is the reason Sarah can't dance in the ballet," I said. "Remember how he put a frog in her dance bag? That's how she sprained her ankle!"

I was starting to put things together now. "And before, when I was talking to Sarah, she said she was a big fan of Danielle Dabro's."

Ashley's face lit up. "So maybe Noah wanted to buy Danielle's slippers for Sarah. To make it up to her."

I nodded. "Remember when we were at the gift shop? A boy wanted to buy the slippers after they were already sold. Do you remember what the woman told us he said?"

"He said, 'I've ruined everything—again,'" Ashley said.

"That's right," I said. "Maybe Noah wanted to buy the slippers for his sister. But they were already sold. So he stole Miranda's instead!"

Ashley frowned. "It's possible," she said. "But where are the shoes? And how did Becky's body glitter get on Miranda's dance bag?"

"Hmmm . . . You're right, Ashley," I said. I thought hard for a minute. Then the answer came to me.

"I know! This morning in dance class—

guess who danced with Becky?" I said.

"Noah," Ashley answered.

"Maybe he got some of Becky's glitter on his hands when they were dancing."

"Mary-Kate, you're the best!" Ashley grinned at me. "Unless . . ." She closed her eyes and started humming the *Nutcracker* music.

"What are you doing?" I asked.

"I'm picturing the whole first act in my head. We have to be sure Peter doesn't dance with Becky, too, so we can rule him out." Ashley hummed for another minute. Then she opened her eyes. "Nope! Peter never dances with Becky!"

She took out her detective notebook and crossed off Peter's name.

"We've solved it!" I said. "Let's go find Noah." I ran out of the boys' dressing room and darted into the prop room. It was a good shortcut.

"Wait!" Ashley called. She came running behind me. "We don't have proof yet."

"Are you kidding?" I stopped and sighed. "We know Noah wanted Danielle Dabro's slippers for his sister. And we know how the glitter got on Miranda's bag. What more do we need?"

"We can't *prove* that Noah got the glitter on her bag," Ashley argued. "We can't even prove that Noah was in the girls' dressing room."

"Oh, right," I said. "Nadia didn't see him in there. And neither did Ariel."

"That's the problem," Ashley said. "We still can't *prove* he took Miranda's shoes."

I glanced at my watch. Mom would be here soon to pick us up. We had only twenty minutes left to solve this case!

"We need just one more piece of evidence," Ashley muttered.

We were both stumped. Ashley picked

up the Mouse King's sword, then put it down. We glanced around the prop room, trying to think of something.

"Hey!" Ashley exclaimed. She pointed to a shelf on the wall. A large wooden nutcracker doll sat on the shelf.

"Isn't that the doll that is given to Clara in the first act of the ballet?" I asked.

"Yes, it is," Ashley said. She grabbed the doll from the shelf. "And it just might help us solve this case!"

"Really?" I was amazed. "How?"

Ashley turned the nutcracker to face me. "See his costume? It's just like Noah's. Black pants and a white jacket with gold buttons down the front."

"So?" I still didn't get it.

"So Noah lost a button from his costume during practice, remember?" Ashley said. "He could have lost it in the girls' dressing room when he stole the slippers. If we can

find it, we'll know for sure he was there!"

"Great idea, Ashley!" I said. "Let's go hunt for the button."

We dashed out of the prop room.

The girls' dressing room was full of dancers. Ariel sat on the floor, pulling on her sneakers. Becky was at the dressing table, fixing her hair. The other dancers were packing up to go home.

"Which color eye shadow should I wear tomorrow night?" Becky asked. "Blue would look pretty."

Ariel glared at her. Miranda didn't even look up. She packed her dance bag silently. Her eyes were red.

"Don't give up yet," I whispered to her. "There's still a chance we'll find your shoes."

"Thanks," Miranda said. "But it's too late. The show is tomorrow."

I felt terrible for Miranda. But I wasn't going to give up!

As soon as everyone left, Ashley and I sprang into action. I scanned the floor, lifting dance bags and dirty towels. No button.

"This room seems so big when you're looking for a tiny button," I complained to Ashley.

"Then let's get moving," she said. "We don't have much time!" She started tossing costumes and shoes aside.

We looked on the dressing table and in the lockers. Ashley even stood on a chair and searched the top shelf of the closet.

But we couldn't find the button anywhere.

"Let's search again by Miranda's locker," Ashley said. "Maybe we missed it. If Noah did steal the slippers, he probably lost the button around there."

We went over to Miranda's locker. I opened it up and looked inside. No button.

"Miranda's bag was on the bench," Ashley said. "Check there."

I got on my hands and knees and peered under the bench. Still nothing. I started to pull my head back, when something shiny caught my eye.

There was a small crack in the concrete floor under the bench. Inside the crack was something round and gold. I pried it out. Noah's button!

"Case closed!" I cried.

THE SHOW MUST GO ON!

I grabbed Ashley and we raced into the hallway. We ran right into Nadia.

"Whoa! What's the hurry?" Nadia asked.

"We found Noah's button, Nadia!" I said.

I handed her the gold button with the Nutcracker Prince's crown stamped on it.

"Wonderful! And luckily, Noah is still here. Noah! Come here right now and bring your costume!" Nadia called.

Noah strolled out of the boys' dressing

room, carrying his backpack. "What?" he asked.

"Go get your costume," Nadia said. "Mary-Kate and Ashley found the button."

Ashley looked right in Noah's eyes. "We found your button under the bench in front of Miranda's locker," she said. "The bench that her ballet bag was on."

"Uh-oh," Noah said. He looked nervous.

"We know you took Miranda's lucky ballet slippers!" I cried.

"No, I—" Noah stammered. "I didn't mean to," he blurted out. "I mean, I didn't know they were Miranda's *lucky* slippers! Or I would never have taken them."

"Noah, why would you do such a thing?" Nadia asked.

Noah dropped his backpack and stared at the ground. "I messed up," he confessed. "I was supposed to buy those Danielle Dabro ballet slippers for Sarah. My mom gave me the money for them four days ago. But I kept forgetting. And when I went to buy them this morning, they were sold."

"So you took Miranda's slippers," I said. "And you were going to write Danielle Dabro's name on them, weren't you?"

Noah nodded. "The shoes she wanted were autographed, so I practiced writing the name. I figured my sister would never know the difference.... But when I heard Madame P. give Miranda's part to Becky, I felt terrible. I was going to put the shoes back."

He reached down and opened his backpack. Inside were Miranda's lucky ballet slippers!

"Oh!" Ashley cried. "We looked in your backpack a little while ago. The shoes weren't there!"

"I hid them backstage," Noah said.

Aha! I thought. So it was Noah we were chasing backstage!

"Come on, Noah," Ashley said. "Let's go tell Miranda and Madame P. Maybe Miranda can get her role back."

The next night Ashley and I got to the theater early. Ashley hurried backstage to get into her costume. I was already wearing my red usher uniform. I passed out the programs before the ballet and helped people to their seats.

Sarah and I walked backstage.

"I'm so excited!" Ashley said when she saw us. "My stomach is doing flip-flops!"

"Don't be nervous," Miranda said. "You'll be great! And now that I have my shoes, I will too. Thanks to you!"

Miranda's mother came backstage. "Miranda?" she said. "I have something for you. A special present, so you'll always remember your big opening night."

She handed Miranda a box all wrapped

up in lavender paper and silver ribbon.

Miranda tore off the wrapping paper and opened the box. Inside was the pair of lavender ballet shoes from the gift shop! The ones with Danielle Dabro's autograph on them!

"Oh, awesome," Miranda cried, clasping the shoes tightly. "Thank you so much, Mom!"

No wonder the woman at the gift shop wouldn't tell us who bought them, I thought. *I'll bet she didn't want to spoil the surprise.*

"You're welcome," her mother said. "Now, go out there and have fun!"

"Wow, Miranda," Sarah said. "You are so lucky!"

Miranda glanced at her mother. "Mom, you know what I want to do?"

Her mother smiled. "I think I have an idea," she answered.

Miranda handed the slippers to Sarah. "For you, Sarah," she said.

Sarah gasped. "Miranda, I couldn't!"

"When I thought I wouldn't be able to dance in *The Nutcracker*, I felt terrible!" Miranda said. "Maybe these can make you feel a little bit better. Merry Christmas!"

"Thank you so much!" Sarah glowed. "But are you sure?"

Miranda smiled. She walked over to me and Mary-Kate and grabbed our hands. "I have my own lucky shoes back. And I have two fabulous friends—Mary-Kate and Ashley! That's the best present I could ever have!"

I looked at Ashley and smiled. Making people happy is the best thing about being a detective!

Hi from both of us,

Ashley and I were having the best time at the zoo. We were part of the Zoo Crew, a club for kids who want to learn about animals—like pandas! We couldn't wait to meet Mei Ling, a panda from China who was coming to live at our zoo.

But the day before Mei Ling came, everything started to go wrong! The goats were eating doughnuts. The parrots were yelling at people. And the snakes were missing from their tanks! Want to find out what happened? Check out the next page for a sneak peek at *The New Adventures of Mary-Kate & Ashley: The Case Of The Clue at the Zoo.*

See you next time!

Mary-Kate Olsen

Ashley Olsen

A sneak peek at our next mystery...

The Case Of The

CLUE AT THE ZOO

"I can't believe that a real-live panda is coming to live in our zoo!" my twin sister, Ashley, said. "Is that cool or what?" She pointed toward the zoo gate. A huge poster of Mei Ling, the famous Chinese panda, hung next to it.

"Way cool," I agreed. "But Mei Ling isn't here yet. The directors of the Chinese zoo have to like our zoo first, remember? That's why Mr. and Mrs. Tang and their son, Shen, came all the way from China. To take a grand tour of our zoo."

"Look!" Ashley said. "There are the Tangs! Let's go say hi to Shen."

Shen looked surprised when we spoke to him.

"You're really going to like our zoo," Ashley said. "And so will your panda, Mei Ling."

"Mei Ling is not just a panda," Shen said. "I visit her so much she's almost like my pet!" He looked sad.

"You'll like the animals here too," I said. "We have chimps, and goats, and parrots, and—"

Shen's eyes widened as he pointed over my shoulder. "Snakes! Snakes! Snakes!" he yelled.

I spun around and gasped. There were snakes crawling out of the Reptile House! Lots and lots of them!

TWO of a kind™ BOOK SERIES

Based on the hit television series

mary-kate olsen · ashley olsen

#32 TWO of a kind Diaries

Santa Girls

Mary-Kate and Ashley are off to White Oak Academy, an all-girls boarding school in New Hampshire! With new roommates, fun classes, and a boys' school just down the road, there's excitement around every corner!

Coming soon wherever books are sold!

Don't miss the other books in the TWO of a kind™ book series!

- ❏ It's A Twin Thing
- ❏ How to Flunk Your First Date
- ❏ The Sleepover Secret
- ❏ One Twin Too Many
- ❏ To Snoop or Not to Snoop?
- ❏ My Sister the Supermodel
- ❏ Two's A Crowd
- ❏ Let's Party!
- ❏ Calling All Boys
- ❏ Winner Take All
- ❏ P.S. Wish You Were Here
- ❏ The Cool Club

- ❏ War of the Wardrobes
- ❏ Bye-Bye Boyfriend
- ❏ It's Snow Problem
- ❏ Likes Me, Likes Me Not
- ❏ Shore Thing
- ❏ Two for the Road
- ❏ Surprise, Surprise!
- ❏ Sealed With A Kiss
- ❏ Now You See Him, Now You Don't
- ❏ April Fools' Rules!
- ❏ Island Girls
- ❏ Surf, Sand, and Secrets

- ❏ Closer Than Ever
- ❏ The Perfect Gift
- ❏ The Facts About Flirting
- ❏ The Dream Date Debate
- ❏ Love-Set-Match
- ❏ Making A Splash!
- ❏ Dare to Scare

Real Books for Real Girls™